A HOLIDAY IN THE SUN

T0316230

Gregory Motton

A HOLIDAY IN THE SUN

OBERON BOOKS
LONDON

First published in 2005 by Oberon Books Ltd
521 Caledonian Road, London N7 9RH
Tel: +44 (0) 20 7607 3637 / Fax: +44 (0) 20 7607 3629
e-mail: info@oberonbooks.com
www.oberonbooks.com

A catalogue record for this book is available from the British Library.

Cover design by Gregory Motton

ISBN: 978-1-84002-520-0

Visit www.oberonbooks.com to read more about all our books and to buy them. You will also find features, author interviews and news of any author events, and you can sign up for e-newsletters so that you're always first to hear about our new releases.

Characters

GENGIS

UNCLE

AUNTY

MUD MAN

HEINRICH

SHOPKEEPER

THREE OLD MEN

CAMBODIANS

POLICE CONSTABLE

With doubling of parts, six actors can play all the characters.

A jungle in the Far East. GENGIS and UNCLE are relaxing on a veranda. A sign reads: SHSH THIS IS THE FOREST-SIDE NATURE HOTEL. *Outside in the Rain Garden a small group, perhaps one or two, aboriginals are strumming guitars and singing 'alleluia' over and over again in a somewhat lost and desultory manner.*

GENGIS: … Everything has a use Uncle…

UNCLE: What fucking use?

GENGIS: Well that varies…depending on…what it is.

UNCLE: (*Burps.*) What about ventriloquism?

GENGIS: Well…it means you can curse yourself in the mirror whilst shaving, without cutting yourself.

UNCLE: Marvellous.

THE BAND: …alleluiaalleluiaalleluiaalleluiaalleluia…

GENGIS: Who are these people, Uncle? Why won't they go away?

UNCLE: They are the old guardians of the rainforest, the matabatabula tribe, little people, pygmies.

GENGIS: What a happy little song they're singing; are they C of E?

UNCLE: Baptists. They help out in the car-park.

GENGIS: Neat.

UNCLE: Yes, they have been cleansed of every error. A people without a past.

GENGIS: They must be really looking forward to the future then.

UNCLE: Yes, you bet.

THE BAND: …alleluiaalleluiaalleluiaalleluiaalleluia…

GENGIS: Tell them to shut up, they're driving me crazy.

UNCLE: I'll complain to the manager. Garçon!!!

Enter HEINRICH, a German. What a friendly man.

HEINRICH: Hi guys. I am Heinrich. Manager of this
forest-side hotel. Everything ship-shape?

UNCLE: My nephew is annoyed by the alleluia chorus
here. Could they persuaded to retreat into the leaves?

HEINRICH: Ah no, so so sad. They are intellectuals.
Inside. Where it hurts. Please. My friends. We must
live and let live. Vegetables. So sad. Please them. They
are a resource. When I took control of this hotel I said
Heinrich, I want to share my knowledge with these
people. They too can share their valuable no doubt
knowledge of the forest and so on with us. We can fly
them to the hospital when they are ill.

◆

A very loud sound of an airliner, the air is filled with fumes.

GENGIS: That was a great holiday, Uncle. In the forest-
side Nature Hotel. I really felt at one with my canoe.
From the moment the jet plane landed till it took off
again.

UNCLE: It was a great flight.

GENGIS: Yes.

Pause.

People don't realise what a great holiday location can
do for your personality. I've really developed. I'm just
that little bit…BIGGER now, and that makes it worth it,
I feel. I think I'll write a self-help book about it.

UNCLE: A smart idea.

GENGIS: Have you a pen on you?

UNCLE: A what?

◆

In a shop.

SHOPKEEPER: Oh no, sir, we don't stock those anymore. I'll have to order one.

GENGIS: Oh. How long will it take?

SHOPKEEPER: Six months, a year.

GENGIS: As long as that? For a simple Biro…

SHOPKEEPER: Yes sir, they don't make them here you see, sir.

GENGIS: Where do they make them?

SHOPKEEPER: Timbuktoo, sir, Katmandu.

GENGIS: I see.

SHOPKEEPER: Yes, sir, they don't make nuffink here no more sir.

GENGIS: Why's that?

SHOPKEEPER: Industrial injuries, sir – thing of the past. So is low wages.

GENGIS: Oh I see. Superb. Progress is one thing we still make in Britain then?

SHOPKEEPER: Very droll, sir, very droll. Only not for export, eh sir? Not for export.

GENGIS: What about a pencil?

SHOPKEEPER: A what? Oh yes, Oxford Street, an art shop. Art R us.

GENGIS: You've not got one?

SHOPKEEPER: No call sir.

GENGIS: What do people do if they just want to write a note?

SHOPKEEPER: A note sir?

GENGIS: A shopping-list or something.

SHOPKEEPER: Shopping-on-line you mean sir?

GENGIS: Or a letter, no…a memo. A love note.

SHOPKEEPER: You want a writing set. Paper, ink, pen, envelopes, address book, the old writing gear. We've got those. Twenty-eight pounds or twenty-two pounds without the envelopes.

GENGIS: But what if people don't want that lot, if they just want a Biro?

SHOPKEEPER: What would you just want a Biro for, sir, without paper? People usually get the whole lot together, saves trouble later on. We cater for all writing needs.

GENGIS: I'll take the whole lot.

SHOPKEEPER: You won't regret it.

◆

GENGIS comes home to find AUNTY in distress being comforted by UNCLE.

GENGIS: I'm home! Oh. What's the matter?

UNCLE: Aunty is upset because a cockroach walked into her living-room.

AUNTY: It didn't walk, it marched; and then it reared up on its hind legs and pointed its shiny black armoured head at me. Oh it was horrible! I tried to throw things at it to squash it but it was impervious and indestructible.

It stared at me as if I was a tiny bug it was going to eat.

GENGIS: Well, never mind Aunty, it probably came in from the Chicken-U-like-SuckUlarium outlet franchise, next door.

UNCLE: Yes, that's right, Gengis. Maybe it was lost.

GENGIS: Yes, it didn't want to eat you, Aunty, it wanted chicken genitals fried in a batter of fish fat served in a big bap with bird-seed on it.

UNCLE: Yes, it's a mistake, that's all.

AUNTY: No it wasn't.

GENGIS: You can't be sure.

AUNTY: It spoke to me! It spoke to me! It was very distressing and humiliating.

GENGIS: What...what did the cockroach say, Aunty?

AUNTY: It told me to change my whole appearance and personality otherwise no-one would love me or even go out with me.

GENGIS: Aunty, this wasn't a cockroach at all.

AUNTY: What was it then?

GENGIS: It was a TV presenter.

AUNTY: (*Gasps in amazement.*)

GENGIS: Yes, it was just one of those programmes where they turn you over.

AUNTY: How exciting. Yes! Yes, it's true, I feel completely made up!

GENGIS: Can they stop you making that dreadful sound when you are being sick in your sleep?

AUNTY looks at GENGIS with indignation.

◆

GENGIS comes in with a take-away.

GENGIS: Uncle, could you resource some sauce for my Tastimeal?

UNCLE: At once, I'll send Jack to Sainsbury's Pakishop.

GENGIS: Who's Jack?

UNCLE: Your Aunty has taken the step of making herself over, as it were, into a man.

GENGIS: Whatever for?

UNCLE: She feels it may help her project a more feminine image. She wants to be an actor and hopes to land a job in a commercial playing a retarded emasculated silly dad in a happy family car insurance ad…

GENGIS: Are you sure the name Jack suits Aunty?

UNCLE: It's better than her first choice.

GENGIS: Which was?

UNCLE: Bobbysox.

GENGIS: Well tell Jack to hurry up with the chutney, my Chicken Wipe is getting cold.

UNCLE: That's not a Chicken Wipe, that's a Turkey Smear.

GENGIS: Oh.

He goes over to a table, strips to the waist, puts on his sunglasses, and sits sipping his cola drink. He reads a large document that has been lying there.

UNCLE: How's it going with the self-help manual Gengis?

GENGIS: Very well actually Uncle. I'm doing the groundwork.

UNCLE: Am I disturbing you?

GENGIS: No, I thrive on the the noise of humanity. It's vibrant.

UNCLE: What's that you're reading?

GENGIS: It's the guarantee of satisfaction and instruction booklet which came with my new Biro.

UNCLE: It's great that these days you can be assured of satisfaction when you buy a Biro.

GENGIS: Yes. And look, it gives some useful tips to make sure you don't come to any harm whilst using it.

UNCLE: Looks fun, good clean and safe fun.

GENGIS: Yes, listen, it's so reassuring:

* do not hold or cause to be held close to any part of the body face hands fingers kidneys liver or spleen or any internal or external organ eyes vagina penis scrotum nostrils fingernails teeth including prosthetic fixtures and fittings of ceramic or non-ceramic compound substances ears knees or throats

* do not lean whistle or sway whilst using this equipment

* do not on any account use this equipment

* if in doubt consult your stockist

* do not use this equipment for any social sexual or political purposes. Any opinions expressed or votes cast involving the use of this equipment remain the sole responsibility of the user. No responsibility will be accepted for consequences of a social sexual political or psychological or economic nature resulting from any such unauthorised use of this equipment.

* do not allow anyone except yourself to use this equipment for purposes of an authorised or unauthorised nature. Any breach of this agreement can result in prosecution

♦ this equipment remains the property of the manufacturer. Any monies fees royalties or other value accruing to the user or any other person from the use of this equipment must be passed at once to the manufacturer

♦ this equipment must be returned on demand to the manufacturer together with any benefits personal social medical or sexual accrued to the user since the time of purchase. Accounts to be rendered on demand

♦ any person who uses or attempts to use this equipment authorised or unauthorised becomes the sole property of the manufacturer for a period of not longer than thirty years and not shorter than twenty-nine years. The manufacturer may at any time remove or cause to be removed by appointed agents any goods chattels children or other persons of the user's household to offset by sale at auction any loss in value of the user due to age or illness up to and surpassing a set value to be determined by the manufacturer

♦ this agreement can be altered or extended to include material goods services or technologies not yet existing but coming into existence at a later time also to include any notions ideas concepts liberties or statutory benefits which may come into effect at a later time than the date of this agreement; any such material or intellectual or legal entities will be said to be tending to the favour of the manufacturer for the purposes of this agreement and its applications

♦ this agreement can be altered extended or terminated without prior notice by the manufacturer. Any such alterations extentions or terminations will be said to be effective in retrospect.

On the other hand it seems rather discouraging. It certainly seems to cover everything.

UNCLE: Don't let it put you off, Gengis. They've got to cover themselves these days. Otherwise people will sue them. Will you start work now?

GENGIS: Pretty soon. The trouble is, I think I need to do more research in the field.

UNCLE: Yes, you've got to have experience, gather some facts.

GENGIS: I calculated that I need a hundred and twenty-seven thousand three hundred and fifty-six pounds to get me to a first draft.

UNCLE: That's a lot of money Gengis.

GENGIS: And then a further four hundred and seventy-eight thousand nine hundred and twenty-three dollars to move on to a second draft...

UNCLE: You'll need some kind of funding...

GENGIS: Self-help books don't write themselves these days, Uncle, you've got to know what you're talking about. People want authentic real-life accounts of actual events and people, and statistical facts with genuine opinions to back them up. I'm not going to be caught short.

UNCLE: We'd better go stateside to raise some money.

GENGIS: Cool idea, Uncle. Get Jack to put herself online and see if she can hitch us a ride.

UNCLE: I don't know why you don't avail yourself of the new technology as well, Gengis.

GENGIS: I think it's just a passing phase, I'm sticking to my Biro. I think the old human values are the enduring ones.

UNCLE: User-friendly technology is here to stay, you...are not. Its benefits are self-evident...whereas you my boy, well obsolescence is a fact of life you are gonna have to face.

GENGIS: Except that I am alive, Uncle, these machines are dead.

UNCLE: I'm not sure everyone would agree with you there.

GENGIS: I have faith in…humanity.

UNCLE: Well, that's very nice, but I don't think the rest of humanity cares for you. They look at their PC on the one hand and you on the other, and they say to themselves: what can this hairy, inappropriate man do for me? The choice is a simple one.

GENGIS: But Uncle, this is terrible. Are you saying you value the benefits of your technological equipment above the inimitable human qualities of your nearest and dearest?

UNCLE: What inimitable qualities would they be, Gengis?

GENGIS: Well…em…

UNCLE pares his nails.

UNCLE: Yes, Gengis?

GENGIS: Well…sympathy, wisdom, judgement, discernment, responsibility and, and…self-sacrifice.

UNCLE: Hmm. Forgive me, Gengis, but that seems to be a list of characteristics that are missing rather than ones that are particularly in evidence…wouldn't you say?

GENGIS: Well, I know that, of late, things could have been a little better, I've tried but, sometimes, you know…

UNCLE: Oh I don't just mean you Gengis…it's the same the world over…

GENGIS: Yes, but still…

UNCLE: If I need any of those down-graded, discredited

commodities you mention, I certainly don't look to people when I want to source them.

GENGIS: You don't?

UNCLE: My personal organiser is very sympathetic, and my Life-system, System iMac Life System, System, is programmed to be at least four-point-five times more self-sacrificing than any recorded human being.

GENGIS: Oh.

UNCLE: So you see.

GENGIS: Yes, I see.

UNCLE: It's a little late in the day for…

GENGIS: Yes, I see.

UNCLE: And the next version, which I have already ordered from my supplier, will be seventy-two thousand times more self-sacrificing…

GENGIS: Yes…

UNCLE: As well as, according to the brochoore, taking it up the arse twice a week.

GENGIS: I guess that's the end of the line then.

UNCLE: It sure looks that way.

There is the sound of a loud fast car outside.

GENGIS: (*He has rushed to the window.*) Oh my God!

AUNTY: What is it Gengis?

GENGIS: That old man was nearly killed by that car going over a red light.

GENGIS rushes out into the street. We hear the altercation from inside. AUNTY and UNCLE stay seated, trying to ignore what they hear.

OLD WEST INDIAN MAN: Hey look at that stupid old fool! Get outta the way of the traffic, you cause an accident innit?

OLD MOSLEM MAN: Shut up you!

GENGIS: Are you alright? That was very close!

OLD MOSLEM MAN: Yes, I am alright thank you young man. They have squashed my plastic bags with all my belongings.

GENGIS: Here they are. Got them.

OLD MOSLEM MAN: Thank you very much, very kind, very kind.

He stumbles away wheeling his crazy trolley full of plastic bags.

OLD WEST INDIAN MAN: You stupid old man, old git! You should do us all a favour and jump under the next one innit? Ha ha ha!! You're mad! What you got in that trolley? Why you wheeling your plastic bags about in a trolley, that's your home is it?

GENGIS: Hey you, leave that old man alone, it wasn't his fault! What are you laughing at him for?

OLD WEST INDIAN MAN: What you aksing me that for? It's none a your business is it? I laugh at what I want to. You piss off! You want a smack in the mouth?

GENGIS: You think it's a private matter shouting at a defenceless old man?

OLD WEST INDIAN MAN: Yeah, that's right, piss off!

OLD IRISH MAN: Yeah piss off you drug addict.

OLD WEST INDIAN MAN: Yeah drug addict.

OLD IRISH MAN: It's none of your business, he can laugh at what he wants.

GENGIS: You think it's alright to laugh at that unfortunate old man?

OLD IRISH MAN: Yeah, who cares?

GENGIS: Well I can see you don't.

OLD IRISH MAN: That's the way of the world.

GENGIS: Because of people like you.

OLD IRISH MAN: Well, if you don't like the way the world is, you can get out of it can't you.

OLD WEST INDIAN MAN: You piss off. You're crazy you drug addict. Leave people alone.

OLD IRISH MAN: Yeah, live and let live. Mind your own business.

GENGIS: But you aren't minding your own business.

OLD IRISH MAN: This man is a friend of mine as it happens.

GENGIS: Aha! So your friends can do what they want, is that it, as long as they're your friends it's alright.

OLD IRISH MAN: Yeah, that's it, drug addict.

OLD WEST INDIAN MAN: You want a smack in the mouth. You bastard.

OLD IRISH MAN: That's the way of the world.

GENGIS: You're a real philosopher.

OLD IRISH MAN: You want some philosophy at the end of my fist.

GENGIS: If you like, sunshine.

OLD IRISH MAN: You want a taste of it do ye, you drug addict?

GENGIS: Don't blame me if you get a heart attack.

OLD IRISH MAN: Oh I won't matey, I used to be the all Ireland kick-in-the-face champion, so don't you worry about me.

OLD WEST INDIAN MAN: It's people like you what makes all the arguments innit? Why don't you mind your own business.

OLD IRISH MAN: Yes, or go down to the cemetry and climb into one of the graves if you don't like the way of the world, go on.

OLD WEST INDIAN MAN: Yeah, you bastard, piss off.

OLD IRISH MAN: Maybe I'll give ye a hand.

We see their shadows upon the wall.

He punches GENGIS who collapses.

The other man hits him with his walking-stick.

They kick and club GENGIS until long after he is unconscious.

(*Catching sight of AUNTY, who is now looking out of the window.*) Have you got a problem with this you old tart?

AUNTY: No, it's perfectly within your rights. I'm on your side, I was all along.

UNCLE: What is it, Aunty?

AUNTY: There seems to be a fight in the street.

UNCLE: Best not to get involved. Just a bit of harmless fun.

◆

Lights back up again, GENGIS is recuperating in hospital, he has been on a life support machine, his head is bandaged.

AUNTY: Gengis, we're so relieved you're alive – We thought it was the end.

UNCLE: And what a terrible end!

AUNTY: Kicked to death for interfering!

UNCLE: Yes, you had better hold your piece next time Gengis lad, you can't say a word to anyone these days before they're kicking your brains out.

AUNTY: You've been on a life support system for over a year.

GENGIS: Have I really? It flew by. Have you missed me?

AUNTY: (*Shifts awkwardly in her chair.*) Well…

UNCLE: (*Shifts awkwardly in his chair.*) Well now boy, how are you feeling, much better? Good. Well we'd better let you go.

GENGIS: Wasn't I missed?

UNCLE: We noticed, didn't we Aunty?

AUNTY: Oh yes, we noticed, Gengis.

UNCLE: Oh yes, we noticed you were gone.

AUNTY: And we wouldn't let them turn your machine off.

UNCLE: No we put our foot down, even though they said they could just as easily make a new one as repair the old. We want the old one, we said… All it takes is a lock of his hair, they said, and hey presto! a brand new Gengis exactly the same but much bettter because less prone to disease.

GENGIS: I see.

UNCLE: But we said no, if there's going to be one we want the old one…until we know more about it.

AUNTY: And the doctor said, you're just being silly.

UNCLE: Nostalgic, he said.

AUNTY: Yes, nostalgic. He was terribly young wasn't he!

She is captivated by the doctor's youth.

UNCLE: I said, I'm sticking with the old one for now, thank you very much.

AUNTY: And he said, 'You old fart, don't you realise a human being is just a bag of chemicals, and if it has the same chemicals it will have the same feelings and if it has the same feelings it is the same? It won't even know the difference…apart from one or two memories,' he said.

UNCLE: He said not to think of your little misfortune as a bad thing, but rather as an opportunity for part renewal. Parts renewal, it was yes, parts renewal.

AUNTY: No, part renewal.

UNCLE: No, it was parts. Because he said, 'If he gets one of his organs kicked out every five years or so he can probably go on forever.'

GENGIS: Oh my God! I'm not a new one am I?

UNCLE: No, Gengis, at least we don't think so… Do we Aunty?

AUNTY: No we don't think so. Would they have done that without telling us?

UNCLE: This doctor, he said, 'You old folk are all the same.' All the same. Get it Gengis?

GENGIS: I don't like this. It means they can make me live over and over again if they want to!

AUNTY: We think it's rather fun don't we?

UNCLE: Yes, it's not bad Gengis. Things are always changing you see. You can't go depending on the old certitudes for ever.

GENGIS: No, but I had rather expected to be able to depend on dying sometime.

UNCLE: Well think of it as a golden opportunity.

AUNTY: Yes it's a great opportunity!

UNCLE: And comparatively cheap.

GENGIS: Cheap?

UNCLE: Yes, it's quite cheap considering…

GENGIS: You mean you have to pay for it?

UNCLE: Yes, Gengis, eternal life, you know, it's not to be sniffed at.

AUNTY: Yes, you have been selected to benefit from this golden opportunity because you can afford it.

UNCLE: Yes, Gengis. Now if you'll look at this small presentation pack you'll see all the benefits that can accrue to you as purchaser, over a period of, say, fifty million years…

GENGIS: Argh!!!!

UNCLE: Broken down into smaller units of course.

GENGIS: Wait a minute. So what this means is that you can have eternal life if you can afford it, while the poor I suppose –

UNCLE: – will be laid to rest. A dignified end is assured to them all. No-one is saying they weren't up to it, they gave it their best shot, but on the day, they didn't make it.

GENGIS: The future will be populated entirely with –

UNCLE: The curse of Poverty will at last be eradicated. Only A-1 Pukka choice will survive, it's better for everyone. A great service to mankind.

GENGIS: I won't stand for it!!!

UNCLE: Exactly Gengis, they chose you because you're such a maverick.

AUNTY: Such a one-off.

UNCLE: An individual, Gengis!

AUNTY: A rebel.

UNCLE: So they want more of you.

AUNTY: Many more.

◆

GENGIS is walking home from the hospital, assisted by AUNTY and UNCLE. He is on crutches and has ataxia.

UNCLE: You have lost control of your limbs, Gengis.

GENGIS: Never mind, it will either wear off or blend in with old age.

UNCLE: You should learn to keep your mouth shut.

GENGIS: I was only trying to uphold a little common decency.

UNCLE: Gengis, your bourgeois little view of life is now terribly out of date.

GENGIS: Oh is it Uncle, how disappointing. What is in its place, if I may ask?

UNCLE: Why, impulse and pleasure alone are real and life-affirming, Gengis, at least that's what I find.

GENGIS: Do you find that, Uncle?

UNCLE: Yes, I do. And I'm not the only one.

GENGIS: But what about everything else?

UNCLE: Everything else is neurosis and death.

GENGIS: You really are a wild, wild man aren't you, Uncle?

UNCLE: I am a superman, Gengis, like everyone these days. We're all supermen, superstars. It's great.

GENGIS: You are a monstrosity.

UNCLE: I work hard, play hard, and shop hard.

GENGIS: And what is your guiding light as you soar these heights of existence?

UNCLE: My own tru-Self is my touchstone.

GENGIS: Yes, but Uncle, do you think this kind of thing contributes to the search for a good and reasonable society with equality for all and fairness and decency?

UNCLE: Excuse me? No, I'm gonna have to take a raincheck on that one Gengis, you see, I'm ant-eye-intellectual, I'm pro-spontaneity, big time.

GENGIS: But Uncle...

UNCLE: Keep it simple Gengis, keep it fresh. I'm a moving target. You've gotta keep moving if you're going to stay out in front.

UNCLE executes a couple of dodges and swerves. GENGIS is rooted to the spot on his crutches.

GENGIS: I can't help thinking sometimes Uncle, that the profanity and banality required of you, as Leader of the Avant-garde, sits awkwardly with your otherwise thoughtful and conservative nature.

UNCLE: Oh do you!? Are you saying you doubt my credentials? Then take a look at this!

UNCLE: pulls down his trousers to reveal a large tattoo on his lower buttocks across his anus of the Nike swoosh and the slogan 'JUST DO IT'.

GENGIS and AUNTY stand looking at it in horror.

AUNTY: Urgh! What is it??

UNCLE: It's a tattoo.

AUNTY: (*Almost in tears.*) But…why have you got a tattoo of a turd coming out of your bottom.

UNCLE: (*Still in his bending-over position.*) That's not a turd, Aunty, it's the Nike smear; all the cool guys are wearing them.

AUNTY: But what does it say?

UNCLE: It says: **JUST DO IT.**

AUNTY: Do you think anyone will want to?

UNCLE: That's up to them. It's a free country.

UNCLE pulls up his trousers and turns to face them again.

So, I think that will silence all debate; no-one I think will doubt my commitment to novelty.

AUNTY: I think I'd like –

GENGIS: I'm sorry I doubted you, Uncle.

UNCLE: That's alright m'boy. Come on Aunty don't you want to be committed to novelty and spontaneity too? It's all the rage.

AUNTY: Well, I don't know…

UNCLE: Go on, it's people-inclusive, everyone can join in; come indoors and with a few strokes of my ink pen I can make your tired old arse a mouthpiece for contemporary culture!

AUNTY: Hmm...

GENGIS: Aunty, think carefully before you do it! Ask yourself: is this ceaseless desecration a sustainable way of life? Where can it lead to in the end? Will there be anything left? Today it's your arse and tomorrow it's your...em...

UNCLE: Look, Gengis, her arse is hardly sacred...

GENGIS: I don't know. It's hitherto untouched... Aren't you saving it for someone, something...?

AUNTY: Well...

GENGIS: Hang on a minute, Uncle. Why are you so keen to make Aunty put a slogan on her arse? Are you on a commission?

UNCLE: A mere trifle, a dime a cheek, we count them by the million, I can take her or leave her.

GENGIS: You see, Aunty, your buttocks are worth less than a quarter of a dollar each, that's about twelve p. You will be just an old finger in an empire of flesh.

They go inside.

UNCLE: Sit down, Gengis, don't get so excited.

GENGIS: I expect you think I've forgotten my self-help manual now that I was on the life support machine? Well it has only made me more determined. To hell with it, take me to the US! I need a sponsor. I'll go and make the sandwiches for our trip.

UNCLE: And I shall go and change. You'd better put on your most casual leesure wear, Gengis. They insist on informal slacks, stateside. Remember it's a republic.

He goes.

AUNTY: What are you doing Gengis?

GENGIS: (*At the fridge.*) I'm reading this packet in case it has important consumer information on it.

AUNTY: What does it say?

GENGIS: It says that the pieces of ham may break…but that this is natural and does not affect the flavour or nutritional value. Can that be true?

AUNTY: If they say so dear.

GENGIS picks up an axe and swings it at a potato.

Gengis, what are you doing?

GENGIS: I'm trying to open this packet now, for our salad.

AUNTY: What is it dear?

GENGIS: It's a potato. It's been vacuum-packed for freshness, naturally, but I'm having a little difficulty releasing it.

AUNTY: Aren't you supposed to cook it inside the packet?

GENGIS: Oh I see.

AUNTY: Uncle did what you are doing with a tomato yesterday, and he got some on his fingers.

GENGIS: Uncle is a child of the sixties. Sadly his generation will soon be dead, and no-one will remember those nature-loving ways.

AUNTY: ?

GENGIS: Yes, Aunty, they will all die.

AUNTY: Die?

GENGIS: Yes, Aunty.

AUNTY: ?

GENGIS: You do know what that means, don't you, Aunty?

AUNTY: Is it something to do with modernisation?

GENGIS: (*Abandoning the subject.*) Vaguely, Aunty, yes. Everything passes, everything changes.

AUNTY: But Gengis, does that mean the present will one day be the past, and no-one will like it anymore?

GENGIS: No, Aunty, most people would say not. The present will not pass or change, the present will go on forever. An endless climax, it is what the whole of history has been building up to.

AUNTY: The people of the past must be so pleased that things turned out the way they hoped.

GENGIS: They're dead now Aunty, but otherwise, yes, this is what they were striving for, this is the end of everything, the culmination. Certainly worth wiping away all trace of the past to make room for, and certainly worth pissing away all chance of the future for.

AUNTY: Yes, this is going to go on forever, just like this. And it's always been like this and will always be like this. We are best, we are the only real ones.

GENGIS: Yes, the rest is just a joke. It isn't real. Except, as I have said, we will die one day.

AUNTY: ?

GENGIS: Yes, one day. Even we will pass away.

AUNTY: ?

GENGIS: Never mind.

> *UNCLE returns in his sportswear, aglow with labels of all kinds from his trainers to his baseball cap.*

UNCLE: Ready you guys?

The loud roar of an aeroplane.

◆

The three get off an aeroplane in the USA.

An airport TANNOY can be heard.

TANNOY: Step back from the vehicle. Assume the position.

AUNTY: What a great flight that was.

AUNTY: So where are we, what's our theme?

GENGIS: I thought we'd go do Brooklyn Pasadena; I booked a package for a power-slimming vacation there.

AUNTY: Yes, I'd like that. I read about it in my newspaper *Weekend Wall of Sound CD-Rom White Noise Supplement.* Apparently the whole of Brooklyn is on a diet, even the mayor, even the muggers and the rapists and the drug dealers and serial killers; it's brought the whole community together.

GENGIS: Isn't that neat, Uncle?

UNCLE: Very tidy indeed.

Sirens.

◆

GENGIS is waiting nervously in an American police station.

UNCLE: Why did you have to speak to that Native American like that, Gengis?

GENGIS: She wasn't a Native American. She was a blond-haired, blue-eyed cheerleader.

UNCLE: But what was her name?

GENGIS: River Between Two High Mountains.

UNCLE: And what did you say to her?

GENGIS: 'Hiya, Popsickle.'

UNCLE: It's looking bad Gengis, you'd better call your lawyer.

GENGIS: Uncle, I've forgotten, what's the charge?

UNCLE: Wife-battering.

GENGIS: But I'm not married.

UNCLE: Yes I did a bit of plea-bargaining for you.

GENGIS: Aha. What was the original charge?

UNCLE: Genocide.

GENGIS: Shall I plead guilty to wife-battering then?

UNCLE: Well in this state they prefer most offences to be tried as wife-battering as they get those paid for by the sponsor.

GENGIS: The courts have a sponsor?

UNCLE: Yes, here in Passadena 'Trim 'n' Slim' County the Justice Department is partly financed by the renowned slimming pill manufacturer – Honesty Incorporated. They pay for all the judges and the hospitality for the juries, and friends of the accused. Very lavish I have heard, I'm looking forward to it, and it's all the more enjoyable when you can be sure of a really good shit afterwards.

GENGIS: Yes, let's not go into that now, Uncle, if you don't mind.

UNCLE: As you prefer.

GENGIS: And on what grounds was the original charge of

genocide made? That chick was probably German.

UNCLE: She claims your remark denied her rights to her adopted racial heritage, and that the verbal rape was an attempt to symbolically impregnate her Native American body to dilute the blood of her offspring with your white, and therefore racist blood, and thereby to exterminate her race.

GENGIS: Perhaps a lawyer would be a good idea after all.

UNCLE: I think so.

GENGIS: Damn, I don't have a lawyer. Shall I try my personal management consultant? Luckily I have his home number, in London, England. (*He dials.*) Ah, it's his Ansaphone.

They listen to the message.

ANSAPHONE: Hello, you have reached the home of Angela and Steve, Carly and Jocelyn, Orlanda and Cleo, Paulette and Muffins, Peaky, Pinky, Peachey. Moona, Poona, Muff and Duff, Holly and Polly, Poo-Poo and Ramone, Sam and Joe, and we all live in a little house called Busy and Smug; this is our family and you are not part of it, and if you want to leave a message for any of us please make it a message for all of us, because we're all equals in this house, please speak after the tone; (*A child's voice.*) Hello? Go away! Go away. We don't like you. Go away. (*Father's voice again in the background.*) That's good, now turn it off, that's right, press the little button, Sam. (*Child's voice.*) No! Don't want to! Shut up Dad. Mum, he won't let me play with the phone anymore!!! (*Woman's voice.*) Oh for God's sake Steve, leave the child alone! (*Father's voice.*) I was letting him! (*Woman's voice.*) Well let him do what he wants with it. (*Father's voice.*) I was letting him, wasn't I Sammy? (*Child's voice.*) No you weren't!! You weren't. Mum, he wasn't! (*Woman's voice.*) Oh for God's sake what's all the fuss about! (*Father's voice.*) There isn't any fuss, is there Sammy? (*Child's voice.*) Yes there is! There is! There is! There is! (*The child is screaming. Woman's voice.*) Of course there is. Silly Daddy, give him back the phone Steve will you? Now. (*Father's voice.*) He's holding it in his hands. Peep peep.

◆

UNCLE comes out of a court room, his shoes echoing on the marble floor. GENGIS in his suit is anxiously waiting.

UNCLE: Gengis, I'm afraid you've been found guilty of wife battering.

GENGIS: What's the punishment?

UNCLE: Indefinite Imprisonment, plus some torture.

GENGIS: Wow, that's unfair! Isn't torture illegal?

UNCLE: Yes but you will be moved to a secret location where you have no rights whatsoever because it is a foreign place and not benefiting from the protection of the Amurcan constitution, and is more like a foreign place for foreigners with no rights, like more what foreign countries are like. You see, part of Brooklyn has been declared a foreign principality.

GENGIS: Which part?

UNCLE: The prison.

GENGIS: What rotten luck. This seems to be against all the rules of decent civilised society upon which Western civilisation is based.

UNCLE: Well, you know what the tough cops and all the cool guys in all the cool films say don't you?

GENGIS: No, what do they say??

UNCLE: Rules are made to be broken.

GENGIS: Yes, well I've always said that kind of attitude would lead to no good in the end.

UNCLE: That's because you are an old fashioned stick-in-the-mud clinging to a discredited past. You should get out more, go to the disco.

GENGIS: I shall do, just as soon as I am released.

UNCLE: That's it, move with the times, read some books, develop some key life-skills, discover Islam.

GENGIS: What?

We hear the VOICE of a nearby sergeant of the court, who has come to take GENGIS away.

VOICE: Step away from the person. Assume the position.

UNCLE: Goodbye Gengis.

GENGIS: Cheerio.

◆

UNCLE and AUNTY back in England. AUNTY is sitting in an armchair, opposite her is UNCLE's unoccupied chair. UNCLE returns to the room, backwards. He is dragging an enormous black plastic bag, with a zip in it.

UNCLE: That was the postman. We have a parcel.

AUNTY: And they've delivered it! How thrilling.

UNCLE: Give me a hand Aunty.

AUNTY helps UNCLE drag the bag into the room.

AUNTY: Whatever can it be? It's very heavy.

UNCLE: Yes, it seems my writ of Habeas Corpus has worked. The Americans have sent Gengis's body back to us, in this body-bag.

AUNTY: Justice has prevailed over brute force!

UNCLE: Let's unzip it.

He does so.

GENGIS sits up. He is alive, but has a black bag over his head.

Gengis! Is that you?

GENGIS: Yes, I had to feign death. But I think that puts paid to any chance of sponsorship. I don't care, I shall go on! Without money!!! Help me up.

AUNTY: Gengis this is so exciting. Does this mean you will finish your self-help manual after all?

GENGIS: (*Who is still wearing the black bag over his head.*) Yes, I've been memorising it for days and nights in the dark. Quick, write it down while I recite it.

UNCLE: Quick Aunty, find Gengis's Biro, it must be here somewhere!

GENGIS: Ready Aunty? Here goes…

AUNTY: Wait Gengis, wait!

◆

Dumbshow. In the darkened room we see only their silhouettes. AUNTY and UNCLE sinking into their chairs, extremely bored and frustrated. GENGIS pacing up and down reciting his book, waving his arms around expressively.

Darkness.

Lights again. Now it is GENGIS sitting slumped in his chair, while AUNTY and UNCLE pace up and down, berating him.

AUNTY: Yes it's all very well to be worried about the pygmies.

UNCLE: Yes, it's all very well.

AUNTY: And we do understand what you're trying to say about…about…

UNCLE: Capitalism, Aunty, that's what he's talking about.

AUNTY: Yes, it's marvellous, capitalism.

UNCLE: And consumerism, Aunty, he's also talking about consumerism.

AUNTY: Yes, consumerism too, I loved that bit.

UNCLE: That bit was great.

AUNTY: And the TV.

UNCLE: And about the advertising, very good.

AUNTY: And of course I also liked very much the piece about… (*Her mind goes blank.*)

GENGIS: …the?

UNCLE: Brainwashing.

AUNTY: Yes, the brainwashing. It's all very well and we agree absolutely.

UNCLE: Absolutely, yes.

AUNTY: With all of it.

UNCLE: We think the same thing.

AUNT: Oh yes, we really do.

UNCLE: Oh yes.

AUNTY: Of course we do.

UNCLE: Of course we fucking do.

AUNTY: But the trouble is, it's all rather…*passé*, isn't it?

UNCLE: Yes, it's a bit *passé*.

AUNTY: Yes, it's old fashioned and we've heard it before.

UNCLE: It's tired.

AUNTY: It's worn out.

UNCLE: Yes, we've heard it all before, Gengis, it's old hat.

AUNTY: Someone mentioned it the other day.

UNCLE: People are always mentioning it.

AUNTY: It's not new, Gengis.

UNCLE: It's yesterday's news.

AUNTY: It doesn't come as a surprise.

UNCLE: On the contrary, we expect it.

AUNTY: We already knew before you told us.

UNCLE: Someone's written a book about it.

AUNTY: Yes, I saw it on the radio.

UNCLE: I got an e-mail about it.

AUNTY: Everyone's talking about it.

UNCLE: We never hear the last of it.

AUNTY: People go on and on about it, Gengis.

UNCLE: On and on. We have to think about it day, noon and night.

AUNTY: It's horrible.

UNCLE: Change the record, son, that's what we're trying to tell you.

AUNTY: Yes think of a new subject before we all go mad.

UNCLE: Yes, we know it all by heart.

AUNTY: So we're going to ask you nicely.

UNCLE: To please not say anything else about it.

AUNTY: Yes, please don't.

UNCLE: Just shut the fuck up about it.

AUNTY: And find something new.

GENGIS: What shall I write then?

UNCLE: You should try something more radical more innovative, more positive, more up to date, something for the twenty-first century.

AUNTY: Yes, Gengis. You must try to get over it, get a life, try to be more cutting-edge.

UNCLE: You can describe the revolutionary benefits which technology will continue to bring us.

GENGIS: Uncle, I'm not altogether sure that I like technology.

UNCLE: Really Gengis, whyever not? It is through technology that mankind achieves its desires. You do want mankind to achieve his desires, don't you Gengis?

GENGIS: I don't really like all the changes that it brings.

UNCLE: That's progress. You like progress don't you, Gengis?

GENGIS: Well, yes…but I'm not really sure I know…what it is…

UNCLE: Progress is mankind achieving his desires.

GENGIS: But what if those desires…aren't desirable?

UNCLE: If they weren't desirable people wouldn't want them, would they?

GENGIS: They might want the wrong things.

UNCLE: If you think you know better than everyone else

Gengis, that's for you to decide. I don't set myself up as a judge of other people's desires, Gengis. As a scientist I am ethically neutral – in fact I am proud to say, I don't have an ethical bone in my body.

GENGIS: But how do we know what's the right thing to do?

UNCLE: Be guided by reason in all things. Is it rational for humanity to try to fulfil its desires? Yes. Is it rational to employ the best means of doing so? Yes.

GENGIS: You must be right, Uncle.

UNCLE: Well now, we've no time to stand around here philosophising. You are just in time to accompany me on a scientific research in the interests of science and progress and pure knowledge and science and academic research.

GENGIS: I love academic research, Uncle, where are we going?

UNCLE: To the Far East, and here are our tickets, expenses paid.

GENGIS: And what subject?

UNCLE: Geology.

◆

The three are standing in a slurry field in the Far East outside an oil refinery. They wear the appropriate green plastic jackets and yellow hard hats.

GENGIS: What an enormous oil refinery, Uncle.

UNCLE: Yes.

GENGIS: Won't it get in the way of your geological studies?

UNCLE: I don't look at it that way, Gengis lad. We have to be prepared to make a few little adjustments to accommodate technology, Gengis, a little fine tuning.

GENGIS: Yes I see.

UNCLE: In fact, that's the keynote of the assignment upon which I am engaged, with my team of other experts.

GENGIS: Where are the others?

UNCLE: Are you ready with the slickometre, Aunty?

AUNTY: Yes, I'm just…focusing it.

GENGIS: Aunty? I didn't realise she was an expert in anything.

UNCLE: Formal studies are not always the guarantee of wisdom, Gengis, in any field. An open mind is often more valuable.

AUNTY: Yes, Gengis, I was specially selected by the oil company for my open mind.

GENGIS: What a dreadful place.

UNCLE: Without this oil refinery, Gengis, you wouldn't be able to realise all your needs and desires and wants. Growth is what we need, Gengis! GROWTH!!

GENGIS: But surely all desires can't be satisfied at once?

UNCLE: Well, no.

GENGIS: Then how –

UNCLE: Some, naturally are fulfilled before others.

GENGIS: So, if no-one choses…

UNCLE: I guess that in practice there is some kind of… queue, a natural order…

GENGIS: And who, Uncle…is at the front of the queue?

UNCLE: Gengis, Gengis, Gengis. Try not to think in terms of competition. What you have to try to understand is the notion of the general progress of the whole of mankind, together – not one by one.

GENGIS: Ah, I see yes. That's a beautiful idea.

A MAN appears from the sludge, covered in…mud from head to foot.

But what about this man here? Surely he isn't enjoying the benefits of technology and progress?

UNCLE: I don't know, let's ask him… You there!

MUD MAN: Yes, Boss?

UNCLE: My nephew is wondering if you are enjoying the fruits of progress?

MUD MAN: Fruits, boss? Sure thing!

UNCLE: Good. He was worried that this oil refinery may have been a bad thing for the people around here, and brought no jobs and ruined all their houses?

MUD MAN: Ha ha ha!

UNCLE: You laugh. Is there some joke?

MUD MAN: Oh yes, very funny joke. Ha Ha Ha!

GENGIS: This man is deranged. Probably they built this oil refinery right here where his house used to be and drove him off the land, and now he lives like a rat, picking up what he can find in the filth and squalor and pollution, and it has sent him crazy. It's shameful to see a human being driven to such depths. Look at him!

UNCLE: Could you tell us what you're laughing at? My nephew here thinks you've been driven mad by your dreadful poverty and squalor and that you are laughing like a crazy-man.

MUD MAN: (*Offended he stops laughing and smiling.*)
Poverty? What you talking, Boss? You nuts?

UNCLE: No, I assure you, I –

MUD MAN: Prime bloody job I got, ya whitey trash, ya
stink a' deadmeat. Pooh!

GENGIS: What's he going on about?

UNCLE: Do you mean that you are employed here?

MUD MAN: That's what I done told ya, buddy boy! Yep!
Prime bloody job. Mm!

UNCLE: Aha! Em…good job, yes?

MUD MAN: Ta cert; is this guy, he nuts?

GENGIS: Not at all, he is a world renowned business-o-
crat and superb economic guru of truth.

MUD MAN: Wow! (*He holds his nose.*) He's high man!
High! Pooh.

GENGIS: We won't get any sense out of him, poor
creature.

MUD MAN: Listen, you junkie! So what you sayin'? You
got two jobs like me huh?

GENGIS: Well erm…actually I…

MUD MAN: I knowed it. No fucking job at all. Y'a bum!
Get offa this land cause I's the scurty gard.

GENGIS: What?

MUD MAN: The Scurty Gard. Chase off the niggahs.

GENGIS: He's a nut. He's…a redneck.

UNCLE: He is, if I am not mistaken, employed as part of
the team of trained security personel.

MUD MAN: Ya! Ya! That's it, man! You got it! See this? See this?

He claws the filth away with his fingers to reveal his T-shirt. It has a Nike Swoosh.

UNCLE: (*Peers at it.*) Ah very nice.

MUD MAN: This is my uniform, and we get it free, man, it come with the job. Prime fucking job, like you never have, ya really stink bad a' deadmeat, I'm telling ya, pooh.

UNCLE: You see, Gengis, the refinery has brought jobs to the area.

MUD MAN: (*Corrects him.*) Two jobs.

UNCLE: Yes, erm – two jobs.

MUD MAN: And I got 'em both!

GENGIS: Alright then…what's your other job?

MUD MAN: What is it? Whaddya think it is?? Jeez! You stoopid or what? Jeez H Christ!

UNCLE: Note the vernacular sounding American he speaks. It seems they either have language classes available to their employees, or what we are witnessing is one of the indirect trappings of wealth; he is obviously able to afford to rent videos and DVDs and watch all his favourite American TV series and films.

MUD MAN: Phooey! Baloney you goddam cripple.

UNCLE: Even if the vocabulary is a little out of date at times.

GENGIS: Your other job?

MUD MAN: I'm the motherfucking Environmental Officer Number One!

UNCLE: That's marvellous, you see Gengis? And what are your functions?

MUD MAN: Ma function, Whitey, is ta clear up tha pallution from da mud. I got a bag a pallution ovah thare. You wanna see?

GENGIS: No thanks.

MUD MAN: It's a ant-eye-pallution policy.

UNCLE: Well, thank you very much for talking to us, we won't keep you from your work any longer.

MUD MAN: That's right. Da sludge building up while we speak. Urgh.

UNCLE: Quite so, yes.

GENGIS: Just one thing before you go…what were you laughing at?

MUD MAN: I's laughing at his joke. Very funny man, this white corpse.

GENGIS: Could you explain the joke?

MUD MAN: Jeez, ya dumb fuck (*As if to an idiot.*) He say local people no jobs, ruined their house, ha ha ha, but man, ha ha ha, these local…people, they is filth. They can't do no jobs man! They too stoopid. Ya think they shovel shit like me? Nah man, they is well too native fa dat! Wow! They is like animals. Ya dig? They ain't cool. Pussies! That's it. Pussies.

UNCLE: I see, they weren't…

MUD MAN: They weren't a quality workforce. Okay?

UNCLE: Yes, I see.

GENGIS: So they brought you in?

MUD MAN: (*At last someone understands.*) Ya!! You learnin', man, you learnin'.

GENGIS: And where are the local people?

MUD MAN: Oh yeah, yeah…y'know I get here and they're cryin' at the fence, 'Oh please boss man, you took our house and land and you promise jobs but where is the jobs?' Ha ha ha!

GENGIS: I see.

MUD MAN: Yes. And I was, like: (*He demonstrates a gesture of disdain and disgust, like a girl from an American comedy soap opera.*) Get outta here! Ya pussies!

UNCLE: Well, thanks for helping us, you've been most…

MUD MAN: S'cool. Nuttin. 'kay?

UNCLE: Okay.

MUD MAN: Yo! (*Holds up a high five.*)

GENGIS: Just fuck off.

MUD MAN: Up yours. Pooh, what a stink!

He goes.

GENGIS: I didn't like him one bit.

UNCLE: So, you see, technology produced in one area, as we have said, to fulfil the desires of one group of people, can be useful to fullfill the needs of another group, somewhere else. We all advance…together.

GENGIS: I know Uncle, it's just that some people seem to feel the benefits…faster than others.

UNCLE: That may be true, Gengis, but it's better than not feeling them at all.

GENGIS: But what if they don't feel them at all? What if they only get the disadvantages.

UNCLE: Disadvantages?

GENGIS: Yes, such as that family of poor people at the gates here, they'd lost their homes, and their livelihoods when they built that oil refinery.

UNCLE: But that other chap, the one who had been able to adjust, he thrived like never before.

GENGIS: That doesn't help the others does it.

UNCLE: Ah yes, now you see there's two points there: one is that they will one day feel the benefits of what is called the trickle down effect, and two, even if they don't, through their sacrifice, they will be contributing to the general progress of the whole of mankind.

GENGIS: Yes, I see. But uncle, can you tell me what is the difference between contributing to the general progress of mankind, and simply contributing to someone else's progress?

UNCLE: The difference, my boy, is if the person in question has a narrow, selfish point of view, or if he sees himself as one of the brotherhood of man.

GENGIS: Yes, that's a fair point, uncle. Fair play to you.

UNCLE: Thank you Gengis. It's firm but fair. Sometimes the truth hurts.

GENGIS: But isn't it a curious paradox.

UNCLE: What is a curious paradox?

GENGIS: That the best path to the progress of mankind is the path created by the desires of the few at the cost of the needs of the many.

UNCLE: Hm! (*He looks askance at GENGIS.*)

GENGIS: Just a thought.

A slight pause.

UNCLE: Yes. Well, it is a curious paradox. A very curious paradox indeed. And one which I can explain in the following way: – Firstly, it has appeared that the best cure for unsatisfied needs is to slowly turn them into desires. The people in the world who spend their time fulfilling their desires are without needs, they are rich. We need to expand that group to include everyone.

GENGIS: I still don't see how it works.

UNCLE: It's all about motivation.

GENGIS: Is it?

UNCLE: Yes it is. You may call it the central mystery of the human race.

GENGIS: Aha.

UNCLE: You could be forgiven for thinking that a man would be best motivated by the need to feed his family.

GENGIS: Yes indeed.

UNCLE: Well, it isn't so.

GENGIS: It isn't?

UNCLE: No. Experience has demonstrated that people are far better motivated by the opportunity to acquire an unnecessary luxury item.

GENGIS: But Uncle, why is desire such a better motivation than need?

UNCLE: The answer to that is the answer to many things, and it is this: – Need is physical, but desire is spiritual; it elevates the mind above the purely animal.

GENGIS: So, by remaining needy, the poor are not only standing in the way of progress on a material plain, but they are lagging behind spiritually as well.

UNCLE: I prefer to put it this way: they are being denied their right to participate in the emancipation and enlightenment of the human race.

GENGIS: That's very beautifully put…but doesn't it depend on what you desire? How about you Aunty, do you feel your desires are spiritual?

AUNTY: Oh yes, Gengis, I always feel elevated when I want something.

UNCLE: It is the very wanting itself, Gengis, which lifts up the human spirit.

AUNTY: Yes, it sets you free, Gengis.

GENGIS: Free from what?

UNCLE: From restrictions.

AUNTY: And restraints.

UNCLE: Yes, desire is like a maiden in chains, Gengis.

AUNTY: Ooh yes, Gengis, it is! I feel like that myself, I am that maiden in chains.

UNCLE: It is an image that speaks to us all, to the whole world, regardless of race, creed or colour, the damsel desire speaks to us all!

GENGIS: And what does she say?

AUNTY: She says: I cannot be kept in chains! Release me, set me free!

UNCLE: Yes, you see, she cannot abide restraints – she will be set free.

AUNTY: Let me go, she screams! Let me go!

UNCLE: And all the people in all the countries on earth

take up the cry, and they cry out too:

AUNTY: Set us free, free to desire, free to live life to the full.

UNCLE: Yes, and all the shackles and chains of whatever nature they be, political, social, cultural, moral, those chains will fall away like so many paper chains until all mankind shall be liberated.

AUNTY: Imagine the day, Gengis! Desire will run through the streets, trailing her broken chains behind her, shouting to all the people –

GENGIS: I can imagine that would be a very moving sight. And what will she shout to them?

AUNTY: Do what thou wilt!!

AUNTY collapses into the mud, exhausted by her frenzy.

GENGIS: (*Helps her up.*) Steady, Aunty.

Pause.

Hm. I'm not so sure it would be a good thing. It could have a terrible impact upon…well all the social services for example…

UNCLE: Ha ha! Gengis, do you realise how middle-aged you are beginning to sound?

GENGIS: Yes, but think of the effect it could have on litter collection for example.

UNCLE: Gengis, Gengis…! (*Shakes his head sorrowfully.*)

GENGIS: I worry about these things.

UNCLE: A man who worries about litter collection as you do is afraid of life.

GENGIS: You must be right, I suppose.

UNCLE: And that fear of life makes you want to repress anyone else, because you are afraid of the life force!

AUNTY: Yes, you're afraid of the Life Force, Gengis! You're afraid of what she will do if she is unleashed!

GENGIS: I guess you're right.

UNCLE: You must try to confront your fears, Gengis.

AUNTY: Yes, you must; it will make you a better person.

GENGIS: Alright, ok, I suppose so.

UNCLE: So, what are you afraid of Gengis?

GENGIS: Eh?

AUNTY: Go on, answer him. Confront your fears.

GENGIS: What…now?

UNCLE: Why let it fester?

GENGIS: Well…it's festered for so long, a bit more can't do any harm.

AUNTY: Set yourself free, Gengis.

UNCLE: And by doing so you will set the world free.

GENGIS: Well, I…don't know, I erm…

AUNTY: Why does the thought of Desire running naked through the streets frighten you?

GENGIS: I didn't know she was naked as well?

AUNTY: (*A bit embarrassed.*) I always imagined it that way…

GENGIS: Oh, well…

UNCLE: More precisely Gengis, why do you think freedom is a catastrophe?

GENGIS: Well…I suppose it must be…people.

AUNTY: People?

UNCLE: What's wrong with people, Gengis?

GENGIS: I…don't like them…

UNCLE: No, you don't do you, and you never have, have you, ever since your very first day at school and you saw other people for the first time, you didn't like them did you.

GENGIS: No, no!

AUNTY: Why that's extremely…racist of you Gengis!

GENGIS: Racist?

UNCLE: And, what's wrong with people, Gengis?

GENGIS: They're…not very nice…are they?

UNCLE: Aha! Now we're getting to it!

AUNTY: Aha! Yes Gengis, you are a misanthropist.

UNCLE: That's a terrible admission, Gengis –

AUNTY: Dreadful. It all makes sense now.

UNCLE: Yes, it all falls into place.

AUNTY: Of course it's a very common complaint.

UNCLE: It accounts for your conservative nature.

AUNTY: It's why you're no fun, Gengis.

GENGIS: Yes, I'm sorry Aunty, I'm sorry Uncle. I guess it is a terrible thing.

UNCLE: Not least for yourself. It must be a terrible strain on your mind in the long run.

AUNTY: Yes, Gengis, it will drive you potty.

UNCLE: It's the tension you see, the inner struggle against yourself.

AUNTY: And everyone else.

UNCLE: The burden of watchfulness and suspicion.

AUNTY: And of being such a dreadful stick-in-the-mud.

UNCLE: The alienation.

AUNTY: The boredom.

UNCLE: Yes, the boredom for yourself.

AUNTY: And everyone else around you.

UNCLE: The loneliness of being an outcast.

AUNTY: And a freak.

UNCLE: In permanent exile.

AUNTY: Driven out for being such a party-pooper.

UNCLE: Always criticising.

AUNTY: And moaning and whining.

UNCLE: All on your own. It's not good for you.

AUNTY: Disliking other people is really just a symptom of disliking yourself.

GENGIS: Is it?

AUNTY: Of course it is.

GENGIS: Where did you get that, Aunty, it's very original and clever.

AUNTY: It was in a book called *Getting Pregnant.*

GENGIS: Ingenious.

AUNTY: Yes, you see your worst sides reflected in other people and you dislike them, instead of yourself.

UNCLE: Admit it Gengis, this may cure you…

GENGIS: Hm. I'd like to, Aunty, but it's not so much that I see myself reflected it's just that I know how horrible everyone is because I'm just the same myself…

◆

UNCLE and GENGIS are walking through the forest. Sounds of birds and monkeys, and chainsaws.

GENGIS: Look, Uncle! Pygmies!

UNCLE: They're not pygmies, Gengis, they're Cambodians.

GENGIS: Look, they're praying to some kind of wood daemon on a makeshift altar made of twigs.

UNCLE: So it appears.

GENGIS: How exciting this moment is for me. I've always dreamed of meeting pygmies.

UNCLE: Cambodians.

GENGIS: One of them is approaching us. I'm going to engage him in conversation. Hi there little fellow!

CAMBODIAN: Greetings Oh mighty master, Oh most wonderous kind American!

GENGIS: Oh now, look here –

CAMBODIAN: Our prayers are answered! You must be from the World Bank, come to save us!

GENGIS: Em…not quite.

CAMBODIAN: Seven moons we have been praying that you would come to help us in our terrible disaster.

GENGIS: And er…what is the nature of your disaster, little fellow?

CAMBODIAN: Well, you see, its like this: This is our forest and erm…we've been living here since Our Father, the sky, pissed into the muddy cunt of the earth, Our Mother, and we were all born.

GENGIS: Yes…

CAMBODIAN: And well…suddenly out of nowhere these other creatures came along and said: This is not your forest!

GENGIS: That's kinda weird isn't it, Unk?

UNCLE: Yes, except you must remember that all property is theft.

GENGIS: Fair point; tell me little chap: where did these other fellows come from?

CAMBODIAN: Well, yes, we wondered also. So we made a few enquiries and the answer we got was that one terrible day, when Our Father, the sky, couldn't find any shade because he had floated too far away from the forest, he became hot and got an inflamed bowel from eating a mountain of rotten cow meat, and that evening he shat a terrible pale pink slime which grew into these other types of men (not very unlike your great self in terms of complexion, it has to be said).

GENGIS: I see. Well that sounds very unpleasant. Don't you think so Uncle, can't we help?

UNCLE: No, Gengis. You see what these types have to understand is that the world's natural resources are not just for their sole use, but are there for everyone.

GENGIS: You hear that? You boys have got to learn to share and share alike. You can't hog the forest you know. You don't own it.

CAMBODIAN: Sure thing, boss, whatever you say.

GENGIS: Good. That's sorted out then. And perhaps, you

see, you can share with these other guys, and, like, do your thing together? Yeah?

CAMBODIAN: Sure thing, boss, whatever you say.

GENGIS: What is their thing, do you know?

CAMBODIAN: Their thing, boss?

GENGIS: Yes, like, I notice that you are praying to a kind of twig arrangement and generally getting along with the wood spirits and kinda blending in with the style. How about these other guys, are they like you? How shall we spot them?

CAMBODIAN: Yes, boss, they're the ones chopping down all these ancient trees and shipping them out cheap to Japan and Korea and Solihull to make them into toilet seats.

GENGIS: Ah, neat!

CAMBODIAN: Yes, boss, they make homage to the shitty arse of the infected bowel of the god that made them.

GENGIS: How about that, Uncle! It's nice to see that nothing goes to waste.

UNCLE: Yes. Which reminds me, I've a touch of the runs. Do you think we can get out of here and find a dry-cleaners for my khaki slacks?

GENGIS: Uncle, there are no dry-cleaners in Cambodia.

◆

The three explorers are now walking along a road, through a village. Sounds of children crying, and chickens expiring.

GENGIS: Uncle, what on earth is wrong with these children? Their stomachs are swollen up like balloons and their legs are like matchsticks, and they are all weak and feeble-looking.

UNCLE: Yes, Gengis, it's a terrible shame, it's a terrible disease.

GENGIS: It looks horrible.

UNCLE: Yes, but don't worry, it's not contagious.

GENGIS: Are you sure?

UNCLE: Yes, my company has done all the research and has come up with the diagnosis.

GENGIS: What is it?

UNCLE: Vitamin deficiency.

GENGIS: Is there no cure?

UNCLE: We're searching all the time. We need some more resources.

GENGIS: I hope you get them. Aunty, when's dinner? I'm... suffering from a vitamin deficiency.

◆

Some weeks later, the three are sitting sipping invigorating health and fitness cola drinks with added vitamins for real sportsmen, on a veranda.

GENGIS: Uncle I've got a bone to pick with you.

UNCLE: Pick on, pick on.

GENGIS: Well, you know those children we saw who were very ill?

UNCLE: How could I forget; what a moving sight!

GENGIS: Well, you didn't tell me they were starving to death and that they didn't have enough food.

UNCLE: I did mention however that they were suffering from the terrible scourge of vitamin deficiency.

GENGIS: Yes, you did, but –

UNCLE: And I have to tell you Gengis I have been working my back eyelashes off trying to get a body of research together around a whole raft of related key issues, not just vitamin DEficency but of vitamin OVERsufficiency too, itself a terrible disease affecting half of the world's population, and one which though perhaps not as fashionable to talk about as DEficiency, it is an issue I for one insist on trying to develop a caring and responsible response to.

GENGIS: That's very noble of you Uncle. I didn't mean to upset you.

UNCLE: It's not always easy carrying the burden of Care, Gengis.

GENGIS: I must say I'm impressed. How is the research going?

UNCLE: Well, I have to tell you, that in the case of DEficiency, there is no evidence of any direct link between that terrible condition and a lack of, what you might call, food.

GENGIS: There isn't?

UNCLE: No. Of course not all the evidence is in yet. Some studies have revealed a link to the weather.

GENGIS: How fascinating.

UNCLE: But we want undeniable proof, not hearsay.

GENGIS: And what about that other terrible disease you mentioned, OVERsufficiency.

UNCLE: Again, there is no single identifiable cause. Some research just coming in suggests that underwear size may be a factor. The larger the underwear the more at risk that individual is.

GENGIS: Large underwear causes Vitamin Oversufficiency Syndrome?

UNCLE: So it appears. We have a programme in place right now trying to persuade the folks in some areas of the globe to buy their underwear a couple of sizes smaller.

◆

GENGIS, UNCLE and AUNTY are standing in their jungle gear in a very large…clearing.

GENGIS: Uncle, correct me if I'm wrong but where this part of the rainforest once stood, exactly where Herr Heinrich's Rainview Hotel used to be, has now the appearance of a recreation ground on Wandsworth flats. Isn't it sad that the beautiful habitat of all my favourite animals and insects is being destroyed? Not to mention the homelands of our friends the pygmies?

UNCLE: I don't know what you mean! Haven't you read the research? It confirms that there has never been so much bio-, and cultural, diversity. The problem is not that there is too little, but that there is too much, so that we may have to cut down.

GENGIS: Really??

UNCLE: Yes. A little pruning anyhow always encourages growth.

GENGIS: I see. And erm…where was this research done?

UNCLE: Only in the most lavishly funded, best resourced, most highly reputable university in the whole of the US of A.

GENGIS: I'm impressed. What is its name?

UNCLE: Its name?

GENGIS: Yes sir.

UNCLE: The name of the university?

GENGIS: Yep.

UNCLE: Why, erm…heh heh…it's name kinda escapes me just at this moment.

GENGIS: No matter, you'll find the name emblazoned on the university cafeteria paper napkin with which you are mopping the moisture from your jowels.

UNCLE: Ah Yes! So it is! Yes, there is is, that's it: The Microwave Supersoft Hardcore Window Shopping Mahogany Toilet Seat Cola Institute of Research/hang-gliding and Related Studies in the University of Las Vegas, Tennessee. A fine body of men and wo-persons.

GENGIS: Exactly.

UNCLE: I don't know what you mean by that.

AUNTY: Yes, what's your problem?

◆

Some months later. Some things have changed. MUD MAN is now dressed in a suit and has a large, open, airy office, high up in a large towering tower high above the mud.

MUD MAN: Come into my office, come and share my space.

GENGIS: Obliged.

MUD MAN: Come and check my window. Tallest muthfuckin building in whole Thailand, baby. You think it's cool?

GENGIS: Yes. You seem to be doing very well for yourself these days.

MUD MAN: Windows of opportunity, man, I broke 'em all. I'm creating forty thousand shit-shovelling jobs man, eating turds from the water system, see those guys it's crazy, standin' neck high in da shit, dose guys is gonna be millionaires like me, in ten years. Or they ain't. If they is dead. Cool?

GENGIS: It's very exciting.

MUD MAN: Tigers. Trickle down, baby. Look at da shit tricklin down! Icy-cool, yeah man. Shivers down ma spine. From dis window I can see more than I want to see. Ya see all dis? – I don't want to see it. It's grimy shit. Ya think I wanna see grimey shit? Getouttahere!!

GENGIS: Should I leave?

MUD MAN: Na, na. Come close. You ma buddy.

GENGIS: Oh thanks.

MUD MAN: Yep. (*He chants.*) Buddy buddy! Up! Up!

GENGIS: Thanks.

Pause.

MUD MAN: Well?

GENGIS: Well, well, well.

MUD MAN: Talk fast shit-head.

GENGIS: Ah yes, now I was wondering…I was hoping to bring up…the matter of…is my uncle hereabouts by any chance?

MUD MAN: Sure. Unky baby! He'll be right along.

GENGIS: I'm here on behalf of…

MUD MAN: Hm?

GENGIS: It's only a small matter.

MUD MAN: It's taking up a lot of time tho!

GENGIS: Hm…

MUD MAN: Hey! I hear you bin helpin' out down in th' hospital?

GENGIS: Yes. Only weekends.

MUD MAN: Ya find a cure yet?

GENGIS: No.

MUD MAN: Sad. Real sad. Keep working on it. Don't give up baby. Sick people everywhere.

GENGIS: Ha ha! (*GENGIS laughs inanely.*)

MUD MAN: Ha! Ha! (*Calls off.*) Hey Unky! C'mon!

GENGIS: Nice office.

MUD MAN: Yes baby.

GENGIS: Much better than your last one.

MUD MAN: (*Stares incomprehension.*)

GENGIS: Haha! (*Laughs inanely and a little nervously.*)

Pause.

MUD MAN: (*Politely making conversation.*) The world's just one big shit-hole, isn't it, whitey?

GENGIS: I don't really understand what you mean, though of course I can guess…

MUD MAN: (*Not listening.*) Lucky no-one has to live long, huh?

GENGIS: What? Oh yes. It's all over in a flash. Now about the…

MUD MAN: What?

GENGIS: Is…Unky about to arrive?

MUD MAN: You want ta talk to Unky?

GENGIS: Yes, please.

MUD MAN: Okay, okay. I get him. That ok? I get him tomorrow.

GENGIS: Tomorrow? But I –

MUD MAN: (*With menace.*) Tomorrow, okay?

GENGIS: Tomorrow will be fine.

MUD MAN: Tomorrow. See if I can. You're gonna shit when you see him.

GENGIS: Am I?

MUD MAN: Sure. He's a real changed guy…

GENGIS: There was a little matter…

MUD MAN: Time baby.

GENGIS: My weekend hospital job…I've noticed –

MUD MAN: The sick people yeah?

GENGIS: Precisely.

MUD MAN: Urgh! Oh! Ow! Oh oh! Oh OH!

He tries to simulate a response of pity, which is more like dismay, then more like a physical pain, then like a trivial physical pain, like a pinching shoe or a sore finger.

Gee, I'm sorry for them, y'know?

GENGIS: Yes I know.

MUD MAN: Oh God I'm so sorry! Oh fuck me! Fuck me, God! I'm so sorry for those guys!

He weeps, nearly, but it is a strange dry, head-bobbing spasm, quite abstract and original.

GENGIS: Yes, thank you, very nice of you.

MUD MAN: S'okay, s'okay.

GENGIS: But…

MUD MAN: Oh JESUS! OH CHRIST! ARGH!

He thumps the table.

Oh! Oh!

GENGIS: You needn't put yourself through so much pain.

MUD MAN: Oh yes! Yes! Yes! Come on God, fuck me!
Ram your cock up my arse until I bleed! Oh God!

GENGIS: No, really, please, calm yourself.

MUD MAN: I can't, I can't, I… I just feel so…uneasy, ya
know what I'm sayin whitey?

GENGIS: I suppose so, yes.

MUD MAN: So dry. It's like I'm up on the cross? Y'know?

GENGIS: I know.

MUD MAN: Please! please! (*He gasps, his tongue hangs out.*)
These people, these people. They take up my whole
screen! And I'm like: what was that?

GENGIS: No, look, you mustn't worry about it, you see,
I've got some good news. I rushed round here…to tell…
Unky.

MUD MAN: Tell ME, tell ME.

GENGIS: Yes well, you see, it seems…it has turned out
that, that starvation –

MUD MAN: Oh yes! Starvation! Oh God yes! Oh! Ow!
Argh!

GENGIS: Yes, but wait, you see, it seems that starvation is
NOT a disease.

MUD MAN: (*Quietly.*) What?

GENGIS: Yes, they told me –

MUD MAN: Whaddyamean not a disease?? What them people in th' hospital fo' den?

GENGIS: Well you see…

MUD MAN: What?? What they eatin' up all th'drugs fo' den? Dem greedy fucks, they ain't sick?

GENGIS: No, no wait, you see –

MUD MAN: I don't know man! Wow! Muthafuckers.

GENGIS: No, starvation is not a disease.

MUD MAN: Oh. Ok. So: What the fuck is it then? Smartmuthafucker.

GENGIS: It's a consequence of –

MUD MAN: 'It's a consequence of.' Smartmuthfucker! Don't give me dat! Consequence. I said: What is it? You Speeekey eengleesh???

GENGIS: Yes I –

MUD MAN: No, you listen to me. The motherfuckers are sick. That's why they in da hospital fo. Okay? So you go 'way an' –

◆

MUD MAN and AUNTY discussing a potential relationship.

MUD MAN: Hey baby, you like it when a man eats your pussy?

AUNTY: Well, I –

MUD MAN: I eat pussy ten times a day, baby. You want I eat yo pussy now, baby? You wet fo me hun?

AUNTY: (*Horrified but trying to conceal it.*) My pussy…is not here.

MUD MAN: Sure it is baby, I can smell it. I luurve smelly pussy, baby.

AUNTY: Would you mind, I think I have to go to the toilet.

MUD MAN: The WHAT??

AUNTY: I need to –

MUD MAN: The restroom, baby! Don't be disgusting, the restroom! Don't go dirty on me baby… So tell me hun: you shave yo lill' pussy?

AUNTY: Certainly not!

MUD MAN: Ok, you clip it. You clip yo little pussy.

AUNTY: No, first a lovely shampoo, then a rinse, then a little perm.

MUD MAN: Mm shampoo and set!!! This I gotta see!!

AUNTY: I didn't…bring her.

MUD MAN: What you talkin' baby? You bein' cute wi' me babe? You want I come an' whip yo pussy an' den eat it? You wanna be pussy-whipped? Honey? You creamy yet honey? C'mon you know you woan it!

◆

AUNTY: Gengis, it was horrible. He wanted to eat my pussy.

GENGIS: Good grief! How did it end?

AUNTY: I had to leave. He fainted.

GENGIS: I see.

AUNTY: He's not very strong, Gengis.

◆

GENGIS: Jemal.

MUD MAN: Call me Tony.

GENGIS: Tony.

MUD MAN: Yes, baby?

GENGIS: I've been meaning to ask you, what is your line of business?

MUD MAN: My line? I have many lines, baby. Man has got to bend, if he don't he gonna snap like a biscuit. You git me suckka?

GENGIS: Yes, of course. A few different things then?

MUD MAN: That's my name, don't wear it out. High five, man.

He raises his hand to accomplish the 'high five' salute of rapprochement with GENGIS.

GENGIS tries to get his hands out of his pockets but he can't. He wrestles with himself, tires, falls onto the ground, onto his face, his hands are stuck. MUD MAN remains with his 'high five' aloft, waiting in a posture of impatient patience.

GENGIS thumps his own face onto the floor, but his hands won't move out of his pockets. They seem reluctant...

GENGIS: I'm sorry, I can't seem to –

MUD MAN: Forgit it, suckka – I was just stretchin' ma arm anywayz...see?

MUD MAN stretches his arm out, it begins to look like a Nazi salute.

See, just stretchin'.

GENGIS gets up.

GENGIS: So you were saying? Your line of business?

MUD MAN: I wuzzn't sayin' nothin', punk. But if you wanna know – it's rest homes fo' da hard a hearin'.

GENGIS: Deaf people?

MUD MAN: Something like dat. Those what don't hear what I'm sayin' to dem, even tho' I, like, say it ten times and dat. Those kinda deaf people, that's, like, hard a hearin'?

GENGIS: Ah.

MUD MAN: So I make rest homes fo dem until they CAN hear what I is sayin'. Loud and clear. Do you get me?

GENGIS: You run prisons?

MUD MAN: If that's what you have a mind to call it, bumsucker, yes. It's a boooomin' business, baby. Come and show me yo pics now honey, you is wastin' ma time.

◆

In the office which UNCLE shares with MUD MAN in the towering block.

UNCLE: What's that swishing noise, Gengis?

GENGIS: Yes, I can hear it too. I had put it down to the tide of fear coming in upon the shores of my mind.

UNCLE: That's very poetic.

GENGIS: It's very noisy. I can't hear myself think.

UNCLE: Scared eh, Gengis?

GENGIS: Terrified.

UNCLE: What on earth for?

GENGIS: Being stuck here on earth…with all the other people. I'm just wondering what they will come up with next.

UNCLE: Have faith in mankind, Gengis. Relax. As long as YOU feel okay, everything IS okay.

GENGIS: Yes, I suppose things can't get much worse.

UNCLE: Actually, I've some very positive news. Our good friend Tony Jemal has thrown over a new leaf. He has discovered his spiritual side.

GENGIS: Oh…

UNCLE: So moved was he by Aunty's phantom pregnancy that he has started a religion of his own, based on his own experiences.

GENGIS: How he must have suffered.

UNCLE: Yes, it's called Worshipping the Man-child. He has the idea from thinking Aunty was going to provide him with a son, a son from whose arse the sun would surely shine, as he put it. He then developed the idea to include all Man-childs, it being an inborn quality among them… us…that the sun shines out of our arses.

GENGIS: Not literally?

UNCLE: Well, I have a more metaphorical conception of it, being originally myself C of E. He has a more concrete view of it.

GENGIS: I'll bet he does.

UNCLE: Yes, it's bound to catch on. I did a rough preliminary market analysis and I found that there are fully four fifths of the world's population who have no cultural, fiscal, social, or theological barriers to the rapid absorption of the idea, it being more or less what they already think. No need for any new trade agreement.

GENGIS: Trade agreement?

UNCLE: So, I've joined forces with Tony Jemal to form the Man-child Corporation.

UNCLE stands and walks from behind his desk, knocking his chair over as he does so. We see he is wearing a long garment down to his ankles, which extends five or six feet outwards behind him in a kind of giant bustle.

GENGIS: Uncle! Whatever are you wearing??

UNCLE: What? Oh this? Well, it's what all self-respecting Man-childs are wearing.

GENGIS: Is it? But whatever is it? Surely it's…the wrong size, or the wrong way around?

UNCLE: No, no, you see it incorporates the Man-child bustle, a symbolic piece of body wear intended to remind believers of the key facts of the faith.

GENGIS: May I…look underneath?

UNCLE: Well, I don't know. There is usually a short prayer first…go on then.

GENGIS lifts the garment to reveal a large wire frame with pieces of coloured paper and material attached to it, like streamers, intended to represent the golden rays of the sun.

GENGIS: It's fantastic…but Uncle, what about going to the toilet? Isn't it very difficult?

UNCLE: We shit where we stand, Gengis.

GENGIS: Oh my God!

UNCLE: Yes, let our mummies clear it up – I mean let the women clear it up.

GENGIS: Oh dear.

UNCLE: This is the way forward Gengis.

GENGIS: In what way is it?

UNCLE: I'll tell you. The Man-child Corporation has already sold three billion Sunshine Dresses worldwide.

GENGIS: I see.

UNCLE: Yes, we're rich. Sales of our fantastic logo are double that, because even the very poorest can afford them. It's a perfect blend of our skills in marketing, budget manufacture and distribution on the one hand, and…other elements of world culture on the other, that provide this fusion for the twenty-first millenium. Would you like to see the architect's design for the clitorectomy clinic, with twenty-five million beds?

GENGIS: No thank you.

UNCLE: Cut their cunts off, and give 'em a shovel. No more head games. Know what the little bleeders are up to.

GENGIS: Don't you think this is a little disrespectful to wo-persons?

UNCLE: Rubbish. It makes mothers of them all – the highest position attainable for a mortal, to shovel shit for Man-childs.

GENGIS: I don't know what Aunty is going to say to that.

UNCLE: She has already given her approval. She says it gives her a dignity and self-respect she has never felt before.

GENGIS: I'm shocked.

UNCLE: Remember how humiliated she was by that TV presenter pretending to be a cockroach?

GENGIS: Yes, I know but –

UNCLE: She didn't tell you that they filmed a whole

second series inside her vagina, laughing at the lack of traffic, taken with a telephotomicro lens without her prior agreement.

GENGIS: No she never mentioned it.

UNCLE: She was afraid you would think she didn't believe in a free press.

GENGIS: It all makes sense now.

UNCLE: She's been pushed too far. Anything which allows her to draw a veil of secrecy over her personal hygiene is seen as a privilege and a salvation. Was there anything else Gengis?

◆

Meanwhile AUNTY and her new husband.

MUD MAN: Oh honey! now you is goin' ta be ma wife, yeah? So, like I want no head-games yeah? And you is like not going with no-one else and you gotta have self-respect and do like I say in all things, and just do yo lil' ting just fo me, yeah, okay baby?

AUNTY: Yes I –

MUD MAN: An' den OOOOHH honey baby we gonna make such sweet love, baby you so sexy, I'm gonna go down on you and eat yo lil' pussy all night long, I give so much pleasure to the womens they all screamin' oh Man-child you is a love machine! – and just to make sure you don' go with no-one else and play head-games with me I's gonna have yo lil' pussy cut off yeah?

AUNTY: But –

MUD MAN: So go tell yo mamma ta bring the clitorectomy towel and shit yeah? D'ya get me dough? And we's gonna have a reeel big party with young girls and sexy, yeah, in dere short skirts. OOOHH I like dem young girls they's so sexy before they get their clits cut off yeah. Oooh yeah soft juicy, baby. Why you so dry baby? You not love me no more? You want me go jiggy-jiggy with young girlies? Okay. S'okay wi' me baby. Take it easy. Later, yeah? I'm outta here.

◆

The office of the Man-child. There is a large logo on the wall. It is made of the lower part of the two orbs of a bottom, from between which are shining the rays of the sun in an expanding fan shape, coloured alternately reddish gold, and yellowish gold.

UNCLE: So, WAS there anything else?

GENGIS: Yes Uncle I've got some wonderful news, I came to tell you as soon as I found out, you see I have discovered that starvation – vitamin deficiency, is not a disease. Isn't that great news?

UNCLE: Hm. (*Pause.*) Let's not be rash, Gengis.

GENGIS: No, but –

UNCLE: Wait until all the evidence is in…

GENGIS: Yes, but –

UNCLE: It's still a subject of some very expensive research by a team of experts.

GENGIS: Yes, but –

UNCLE: All paid for by industry Gengis, as we go forwards into the next millennium, searching for a high technology solution to create a better world for the twenty-first …em millen…the thousand and first centu…the future. You don't want to stand in the way of that, do you Gengis?

GENGIS: No, of course not, but –

UNCLE: We are on the brink of a discovery that will render obsolete all previous…ideas on this matter, creating as it will, a superabundance of…vitamin sources, in easily available forms which will remain the intellectual property of the manufacturer thus guarding against abuse.

GENGIS: Yes, I know Uncle, but –

UNCLE: But what, Gengis?

GENGIS: Well it seems…that since…vitamin deficiency is not a disease, that it can be cured by sharing out the cake, as it were…

UNCLE staggers slightly, caused by a brief fainting-fit, from which he recovers with fortitude. He begins to pace up and down, still wearing his Sunshine Dress with its giant bustle.

UNCLE: Ah yes, what you have in mind is a re-allocation of resources. It's not that simple, Gengis.

GENGIS: Well, no of course, but –

UNCLE: It doesn't work like that.

AUNTY: If only it did.

UNCLE: Yes, if only it did.

AUNTY: But it doesn't.

UNCLE: There isn't any cake, Gengis.

AUNTY: There's no such thing.

UNCLE: It's a false analogy.

AUNTY: It's not like that.

UNCLE: Cake is finite.

AUNTY: Whereas…em.

UNCLE: Prosperity is infinite.

AUNTY: It's endless, limitless, there's as much as you like.

UNCLE: Theoretically

AUNTY: Of course.

UNCLE: So, there's no need to worry about sharing it out, but rather we need to just make some more.

AUNTY: It's better for everyone, Gengis.

UNCLE: And we need to see to it that, to keep up the analogy, that everyone in the world can make their own cake, rather than hoping for some of ours.

AUNTY: We don't want that AND it's very bad for them.

UNCLE: They have to make their own.

AUNTY: LET THEM MAKE CAKE!!!

UNCLE: Precisely, Aunty.

AUNTY: And in the meantime we can make a lot more cake for ourselves.

UNCLE: Yes, try to see the world as a kind of a giant cake kitchen: the important thing is that nothing stands in the way of us all working together, in harmony, to make as much cake as possible. It's all about Access.

GENGIS: Access to…?

UNCLE: …the kitchen, other parts of the kitchen, other kitchens, all the saucepans, other people's saucepans, tables and chairs, meat-cleavers, and the little chefs.

AUNTY: Vegetable chefs, the ones that do the chopping, we need hundreds of millions of them.

GENGIS: I see, we don't already have enough access?

UNCLE: We have some, but not all. We need all the access. If we had that all the problems would be solved. We would all have access to each other.

GENGIS: It's that last bit of denied access that accounts for everything being not quite as it should?

UNCLE: That's it. We need unlimited access, Gengis, no impediments. A level playing-field.

AUNTY: A clear work-top.

UNCLE: Then we need people to eat the cake.

AUNTY: We need access to them as well, Gengis, otherwise what's the point?

GENGIS: I'm a bit lost.

UNCLE: It's simple, Gengis.

GENGIS: I don't know… Won't they be eating their own cake, that Aunty said they had to make?

UNCLE: They might be, but that doesn't mean we can't get them to eat ours as well.

AUNTY: Or instead.

UNCLE: Ours is easier to digest.

AUNTY: It's light and airy.

UNCLE: There's almost nothing in it.

GENGIS: Won't they…get fat?

UNCLE: They may do, and if they dont we'll stuff the fucking cake down their throats until they ARE bloody fat, until their guts are as big as I want them to be!!!

GENGIS: Uncle! Calm down.

UNCLE: What I mean is, it's in all our best interests.

AUNTY: We need more of everything.

UNCLE: Which is why we need research into a MODERN solution for today's kinda world, to leave behind the old fashioned issues of…

GENGIS: – sharing out the…

UNCLE: …cake, and concentrate instead…on jam.

GENGIS: Jam?

UNCLE: Yes, jam tomorrow.

GENGIS: Oh. But –

UNCLE: Remembering of course that tomorrow always comes sooner than you imagine, and look forwards to a better, brighter, more shiny surface, I mean future, a more shiny future that only technology can bring.

GENGIS: It's all very confusing.

UNCLE: The best, most natural theories are sometimes… hard to grasp

GENGIS: Well, yes. But can't we, in the meantime –

UNCLE: I'll tell you what though, Gengis. There is one very distinct and immediate advantage we can take from your wonderful discovery that vitamin defieciency is not a disease.

GENGIS: Oh good. What is that?

UNCLE: We can close the hospitals.

AUNTY: Gengis, there are some…people pressing their faces up against the glass wall.

GENGIS: Show them in, Aunty, show them in.

The CAMBODIANS are shown into the office.

Ah yes, do come in, step right this way. How nice to see you all!

CAMBODIAN: It is nice to be in Heaven, thank you.

GENGIS: However did you find me here?

CAMBODIAN: We followed the sign.

GENGIS: Oh, and what sign was that?

CAMBODIAN: The one that is there on the wall, and that is also outside the building and on the chests and bottoms of all peoples everywhere.

GENGIS: This you mean? Uncle's Man-child logo?

CAMBODIAN: The sign of the infected bowel, yes.

GENGIS: But...no, no, you've got it wrong.

CAMBODIAN: Look, here is the great arse of God, and here is the terrible pinky yellow slime from the infected bowel. We knew we would find you and your friends and the great wise man there.

GENGIS: Well, how can I help you?

CAMBODIAN: Oh master! master! Oh great American from the World Trade Organ come to help us, the terrible sly one of the infected bowel is burning down our forest.

GENGIS: Oh, no surely not, perhaps he is making some charcoal for a Barbie Queue.

CAMBODIAN: No master, he has hundreds of men with him with petrol cans setting fire.

GENGIS: I see. I always thought he was unstable. I will telephone the police at once.

They start to leave.

Won't you wait one moment while I telephone?

CAMBODIAN: No, we must go back and roll in the flames to atone for not saving the forest, the honourable pubic hair of Our Mother, the earth. If she is to be denuded and shaved then we must die like flat lice.

GENGIS: I'm terribly sorry.

CAMBODIAN: Never mind guv'nor.

GENGIS: I'll stop it as soon as I can. My Aunty will show you out.

AUNTY: This way please gentlemen.

GENGIS: Uncle, you see! Tony Jemal is setting light to the forest!!! I must call the police at once!

UNCLE: Oh dear, well, I shouldn't worry, Gengis, it will… burn itself out…eventually.

GENGIS: But Uncle, Aunty! What about the pygmies? Their little altar made of twigs…

UNCLE: Actually, Gengis, I think you'll find that pygmies are cannibals and eat their children. I wouldn't trouble yourself about them. Mankind must move on. Personally I hate the sight of blood.

AUNTY: Oh yes, Gengis, none of us would like to be strapped naked to a table and sacrificed.

GENGIS: I… I didn't know…they seem quite nice to me.

UNCLE: Have you actually met any pygmies, Gengis?

GENGIS: Well, no, I… I haven't met any but…there were those…Cambodians.

UNCLE: Ah well, that's another matter.

AUNTY: Oh well if you haven't met any pygmies, Gengis…

UNCLE: Don't you think you're being a bit sentimental?

AUNTY: Oh yes, Gengis, you mustn't be sentimental. You might end up making a terrible, terrible mistake.

GENGIS: Like what?

AUNTY: I don't know, you might end up…unnecessarily

getting in the way of…something that's happening… when you needn't have…bothered.

GENGIS: I see.

AUNTY: And that would be awful.

GENGIS: Look, never mind about the pygmies, Tony Jemal has gone crazy I'd better go and stop him.

UNCLE: Don't be too hard on the boy, Gengis.

AUNTY: You don't understand him.

GENGIS: Don't I?

AUNTY: No, you've got him all wrong.

UNCLE: You see, it's alright for you, Gengis, but this boy is fighting against poverty.

GENGIS: He seems to be doing alright to me.

UNCLE: It may seem like that to you, Gengis.

AUNTY: …but don't be fooled by appearances.

UNCLE: He's in hock right up to his eyeballs.

AUNTY: It's dreadful, Gengis! My poor husband!!

UNCLE: Aunty's home-life is suffering as a consequence.

AUNTY: He's working all hours, Gengis.

GENGIS: Who is his major creditor?

UNCLE: Ahem…well, I'm giving him the most favourable terms I can…

GENGIS: Well, I'm sorry but I don't see what –

AUNTY: How is he ever going to pay it all off???!!!!

UNCLE: We're doing all we can for him Gengis, but you seem to want to keep him in poverty, face down in the mud where we found him.

AUNTY: Oh Gengis, why do you want to condemn him to eternal poverty and keep him face down in the mud!

UNCLE: Yes, Gengis what right do you have to deny a poor man his share of happiness?

AUNTY: It's alright for you, Gengis, you've got everything you could ever dream of.

UNCLE: It's a rotten attitude, Gengis.

AUNTY: So mean.

UNCLE: Pull up the ladder, Jack, I'm alright.

GENGIS: I just…don't see the point.

UNCLE: Not a very strong argument, Gengis.

GENGIS: So…why IS he setting fire to…the kitchen?

UNCLE: He's expressing his negativity, and who can blame him? It's hell being in debt.

AUNTY: He's exploring his dark side.

UNCLE: He's an individual, Gengis, just like everyone else.

AUNTY: It's his moody side, Gengis.

UNCLE: It's consistent with the character profile of a goal-motivated target achiever.

AUNTY: He's saying, 'I'm me, I'm ok. Do you have a problem with that?'

UNCLE: And I don't have a problem with that, do you Aunty?

AUNTY: No, it's no problem at all.

UNCLE: Maybe, Gengis, YOU should look inside yourself at whatever is in there and ask yourself: 'Why am I like this?'

AUNTY: And then get back to us.

GENGIS: Can you smell petrol? Can you smell smoke?
Maybe I should make the call anyway…

He takes up the phone.

*We can hear the police telephone operator, a CONSTABLE,
as well as GENGIS, but we miss GENGIS's first words.*

CONSTABLE: (*On the telephone.*) …arson you say, sir? And
what proof do you have?

GENGIS: Well, I…

CONSTABLE: Has he lit the fires yet, sir?

GENGIS: I don't know, maybe not. He's about to.

CONSTABLE: Well then…

GENGIS: Yes but…

CONSTABLE: So, what you're saying is…no crime has
been committed.

GENGIS: Well, no not yet, but –

CONSTABLE: And no-one has been hurt.

GENGIS: Not yet no, would you like there to be?

CONSTABLE: There's nothing we can do about it.

GENGIS: Why not?

CONSTABLE: To be honest with you sir, this type of thing
isn't a priority.

GENGIS: That's riduculous.

CONSTABLE: You tell your MP that sir.

GENGIS: That's not much use now is it.

CONSTABLE: You could try the council.

GENGIS: I'll write them a letter about it on Monday, meanwhile...

CONSTABLE: Or I can put you through to the command and control resources force control unit, at Basildon.

GENGIS: Basildon?? What will they do?

CONSTABLE: Well, nothing now, sir, they're closed until Monday.

GENGIS: Okay give me the local police station. They are bound to want to help, because I can see now, they are actually on fire themselves.

CONSTABLE: What station is it?

GENGIS: Stickyville.

CONSTABLE: Putting you through.

GENGIS: Hello.

CONSTABLE: Hello.

GENGIS: It's you again isn't it?

CONSTABLE: Yes sir.

GENGIS: I wanted Stickyville.

CONSTABLE: This is Stickyville.

GENGIS: Are you inside Stickyville police station?

CONSTABLE: No.

GENGIS: Where are you?

CONSTABLE: Basildon.

GENGIS: I wanted Stickyville.

CONSTABLE: It's a central number, it covers every station in the southern and northern hemispheres.

GENGIS: Can you contact the officers at Stickyville and tell them that their building is on fire?

CONSTABLE: No, I couldn't do that sir. I can put you through to the Force Resource Control Command Source Resource Control Unit.

GENGIS: Where's that?

CONSTABLE: That's here sir.

GENGIS: That's you again is it?

CONSTABLE: Shall I put you through?

GENGIS: Okay.

CONSTABLE: Good evening. What's the nature of your call?

GENGIS: Well, it's…

CONSTABLE: Do you wish to report a crime sir?

GENGIS: I don't know…yes.

CONSTABLE: Okay.

GENGIS: Hello.

CONSTABLE: Hello. State the nature of the call please.

GENGIS: I wish to report a crime.

CONSTABLE: Theft, murder or rape?

GENGIS: Em…arson.

CONSTABLE: Theft, murder or rape?

GENGIS: It's more like arson.

CONSTABLE: That will come under parking. I'll put you through.

GENGIS: NO!

CONSTABLE: Parking.

GENGIS: Hello, yes I'd like to report a fire.

CONSTABLE: You want the fire brigade.

GENGIS: Okay. Could you –

CONSTABLE: Hello? Fire brigade.

GENGIS: Arson! Arson! Help!!

CONSTABLE: Arson, sir? You want the police for that.

GENGIS slams down the phone.

GENGIS: Good God! We'll have to take direct action.

UNCLE: That's right Gengis. You can be a have-a-go-hero.

GENGIS: I'm not tough enough.

UNCLE: No, well you've got to be tough to take the law into your own hands.

GENGIS: Yes.

UNCLE: You've got to be hard. A real hard nut. A real fucking nutter.

GENGIS: Law-enforcing citizens.

UNCLE: Yes, real hard nuts.

GENGIS: Luckily there are some real hard nuts around, to keep law and order.

UNCLE: Yes, the type who can deal out a bit of rough house.

GENGIS: Smack 'em up a bit.

UNCLE: Go in hard and kick the shit right out of them.

GENGIS: Unlimited violence.

UNCLE: Kick their fucking brains out.

GENGIS: Someone who speaks their language.

UNCLE: It's the only language they understand.

GENGIS: The language of crime.

UNCLE: Yes, we need people who speak the language of crime.

GENGIS: Criminals.

UNCLE: Yes we need criminals to take the law into their own hands. There's a likely looking lad, I'll go and have a word.

GENGIS: But, Uncle, that's Tony Jemal.

UNCLE: Yes, he's just the man for the job.

The flames surge, crackling and burning.

◆

A factory burning down. Screams. Subsides. Embers.

GENGIS: A shoe factory, no fire escapes apparently.

UNCLE: Apparently not.

GENGIS: I counted forty charred corpses, Uncle.

UNCLE: Forty eh? Don't worry, they will have suffocated rather than burnt.

GENGIS: Whose shoes?

UNCLE: Whose shoes?

GENGIS: Whose shoes.

UNCLE: It is the manufactory of my favourite brand of training-shoe, indeed. I swear by them, in fact I wouldn't be seen dead wearing anything else. Did you know they allow your feet to breathe by a scientifically developed system of making holes in the plastic. Feet must be allowed to breathe, you see, Gengis.

GENGIS: I didn't mean that.

UNCLE: Who owns the factory? Is that what you mean?

GENGIS: Precisely.

UNCLE: Well, of course, I don't own it. I don't actually own any factories. Except my special showcase social welfare centres of excellence and happy workers in Taiwan. Would you like a guided tour? We encourage criticism, it makes us work even harder to achieve perfection. Shinier floors you've never seen.

GENGIS: Not now thanks, Uncle.

UNCLE: It is Tony Jemal who owns this factory. It's him I feel sorry for.

GENGIS: Why's that?

UNCLE: He was carrying out a special order for me, working as hard as ever he could to produce, not just shoes, but an emergency consignment of, well…you won't believe this.

GENGIS: Won't I?

UNCLE: Biros.

GENGIS: Biros.

UNCLE: Your little experience made me think there was a small hole in the market.

GENGIS: It's a terrible sight.

UNCLE: But if you look around you Gengis, you will see also the great prosperity the factory has brought.

GENGIS: (*Vaguely.*) What prosperity?

UNCLE: It's unstoppable! Let it cost what it may! If you

want a Biro, Gengis, this is what it costs to produce it.

GENGIS: I'm willing to try a pencil.

UNCLE: Graphite and wood, to produce it you have to –

GENGIS: Or a quill.

UNCLE: It's no good, Gengis. If you want anything, you want it all. So cheer for every inch of vegetation replaced with good sound concrete, weep tears of joy for every tree that is felled, it's all done for you Gengis. Every word of your self-help manual needs the sweat of a Filipino girl, just as she depends in turn on a thousand others of her own kind, until, standing on each other's shoulders, they make a pile high enough for one of them to see over the wall into the promised land. And then, held aloft in triumph, she will cry out, 'Four generations we have worked towards this moment, but at last we have arrived! And we know what we must do now don't we? Yes! CONSUME! Consume as no-one has ever consumed before!!!! Consume! CONSUME!' Because you see Gengis, we all want the same. And we must beware, for it is a battle, a war, a war to consume as much as possible, and the less you consume the more the others consume. And if you let them consume more than you, you will become their slaves. You will make their shampoo for them, and they will breathe YOUR air. And we don't want to end up like that. And so I say to you, Gengis: – Go shopping! Go shopping for your country, go shopping for your children, for your aged parents, go shopping, for the old, the sick, the weak, the frail of mind, the hard of hearing, the mentally handicapped, go shopping to save them, to bring them health and prosperity; if you believe in municipal gardens go shopping, if you believe in beautiful churches and mosques to worship the great gardener – go shopping. Buy whatever you can, buy whatever they want you to buy, don't quibble about what it is, you'll find some use for it. Squirt it somewhere, anywhere, up your arse, behind the fridge, in your children's mouths and eyes! It's an emergency! Squirt it, use it, drink it, eat it, break it and buy it again, use as much air and earth and wind and fire as you can, keep the earth spinning or it will stop, keep the fires burning or they will go out, keep the engine running or it will stall, and if the steering breaks, rip it out and throw it into the road, and if the driver dies push him out, but for God's sake keep the wheels rolling; if a wall appears in front of you, pick up speed and hit it as hard and as fast as possible, and may God grant that the sparks fly high and the heat from the bending and breaking of iron and steel will ignite your flesh and bones so that they in turn provide heat for the fire, and when that is gone, let the ashes store embers for the fire, until there is nothing left, until all has been consumed and we were warm until the very end, until the last faint spark flickered away into blackness.

End.